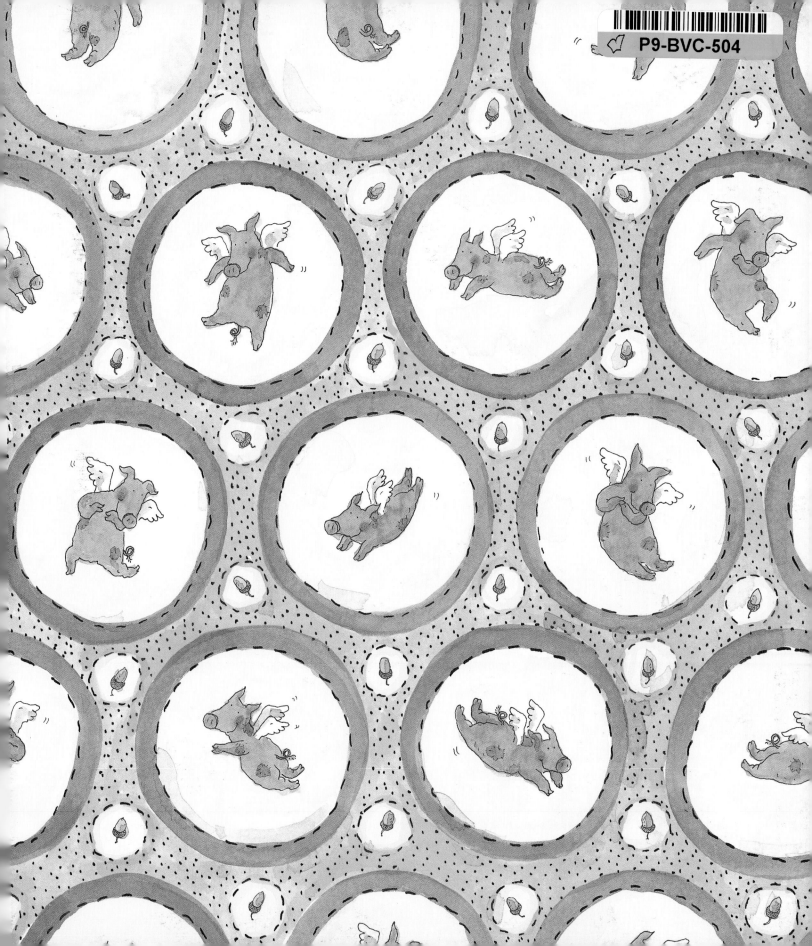

The Pig Who Wished

Joyce Dunbar ☆ Illustrated by Selina Young

DK

A DK PUBLISHING BOOK
www.dk.com

First American Edition, 1999
2 4 6 8 10 9 7 5 3

Published in the United States by DK Publishing, Inc.
95 Madison Avenue, New York, New York 10016

Text copyright © 1999 Joyce Dunbar
Illustrations copyright © 1999 Selina Young

Printed in Hong Kong by Wing King Tong

Library of Congress Cataloging-in-Publication Data
Dunbar, Joyce.
The pig who wished / written by Joyce Dunbar: illustrated by Selina Young
– 1st American ed.   p.   cm. – (DK toddlers storybook)
Summary: When a pig swallows a magic acorn, all her wishes come true.
ISBN 0-7894-3487-3 (Hardback)
ISBN 0-7894-4599-9 (Paperback)
[1. Pigs–Fiction. 2.Wishes–Fiction.]
I. Young, Selina, ill. II. Title. III. Series.
PZ7.D8944P1   1998
[E] – dc21   98-28832
                                    CIP
                                    AC

Once there was a pig who swallowed a magic acorn so that all of her wishes came true.

"oh, I do wish I could get out of my Pigpen and Look at the stores," said the pig.

piggy Place

And the pig did get out of her pigpen,
and she did look at the stores.
And nobody minded one bit!

"Oh, I do wish I could go into that tea shop and have a pot of tea and a plate of cream puffs," said the pig.

And the pig did go into the tea shop, and she did have a pot of tea and a plate of cream puffs. And nobody minded one bit!

Then a baby went by in a stroller.

The baby held a cuddly toy pig.

"Oh, I do wish I could ride home with that baby in his stroller and share all his toys," said the pig.

And *the* pig did r*i*de *home* with the baby in his stroller, and she did s*h*are his toys.
And nobody minded one bit!
Then the baby's mommy said, "**Bathtime!**"

"oh, I do wish I could play with that baby in his bath and make a big Splash!" said the pig.

And the pig did play with the baby in his bath, and they did make a big Splash! And nobody minded one bit! Then the baby's daddy came along and said, "Bedtime!"

"Oh, I do wish I could have a piggy-back ride with that baby and be tucked into a warm cozy bed," said the pig.

And the pig did get a piggy-back ride with the baby, and she was tucked into a warm cozy bed. And nobody minded one bit!

Then the baby's mommy and daddy said,
"Sleepytime!"

The pig settled down to *try* to sleep but the baby "bounced" around on the bed. So the pig *bounced* around with the baby.

"Oh, I do wish my two little brothers were here, too.
We could all bounce around with the baby,"
said the pig.

And suddenly *the* p*i*g's two little brothers were there, too. And they all bounced around with the baby. And nobody minded one bit!

"Oh, I do wish that lady from the tea shop could come and bounce, too," said the pig.

And the lady from the tea shop did come, and she bounced on the bed with the baby and the three little pigs. And nobody minded one bit!

"Oh, I do wish that mommy and daddy would join in," said the pig.

And the baby's *mommy* and *daddy* did join in.
They bounced on the bed with the lady from the
tea shop and the baby and the three little pigs.

BOUNCE!

Onto the bed.

BOUNCE! Up to the ceiling.

CRASH! Right through the floor.

The pig was so surprised, she hiccuped.

Out of her mouth popped the magic acorn so that her wishes no longer came true.

Hiccup!

And when the baby's mommy and daddy saw that they had **bounced** through the floor with the lady from the tea shop and the baby and the three little pigs, they did mind. They minded a lot!

"**Shoo!**" they shouted at once.

But the baby still didn't mind, not one bit.

Neither did the pig.

for Sarah, Gregory,
and Russell ~ J.D.

for Georgina and
Angus Darling ~ S.J.

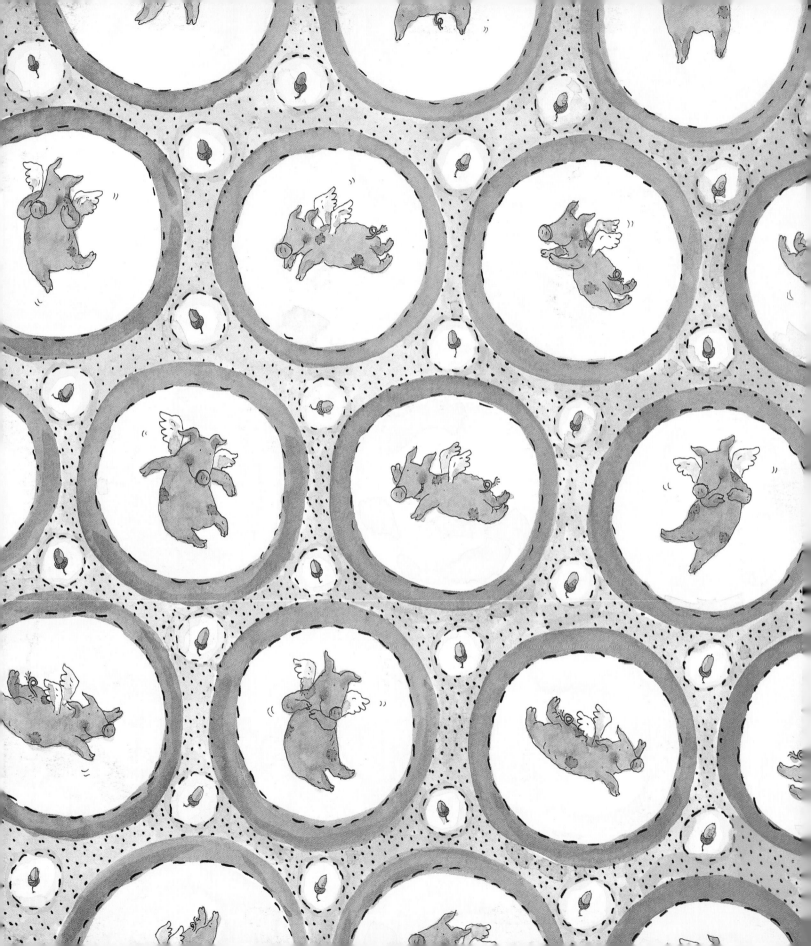